# Sir Cannoli in the Lands of Cavall

This book is dedicated to all the lovers of pups and a nod to the felinophiles.

# Puns, Word Play, & Definitions

clawful - awful
cat-astrophe - catastrophe
dachshund - dach-sund - wiener dog
Feline Fine - Feeling Fine
furever - forever
furget - forget
furprise! - surprise!
kitten me - kidding me
meowment - moment
meowntains - mountains
pawlite - polite
pawsionate - passionate
pawsitive - positive
pawsible! - possible!
pawsome - awesome
shih tzu - shee dzoo - toy dog
ruff - rough
ruff pooches - rough patches

Once upon a time, there was a Corgi named Sir Cannoli the Sploot.

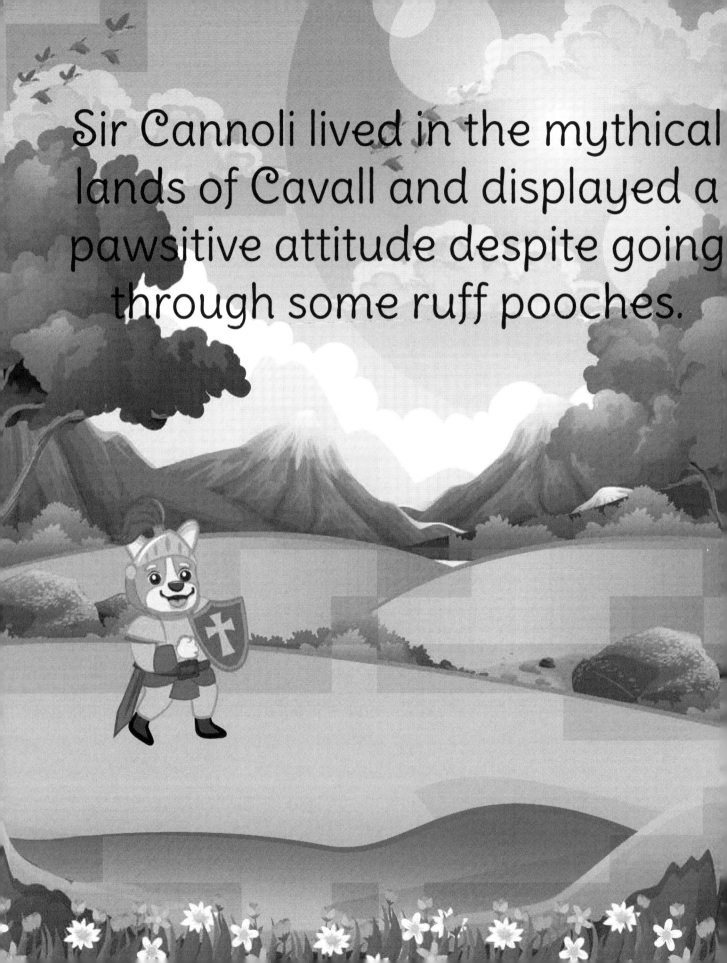

Sir Cannoli lived in the mythical lands of Cavall and displayed a pawsitive attitude despite going through some ruff pooches.

Sir Cannoli prepares for his pawsome adventure to find Fortress Furball.

Hidden amongst the trees, two cats from the clawful Feline Fine Furever Crew wait

for the right meowment to cause a cat-astrophe.

Skitter and Scatter
scramble for the woods!

Sir Pugsley the Pawlite and Sir Andouille the Pawsionate arrive in a flash.

Proudly, Pugsley exclaims, "I am Sir Pugsley the Pawlite. I Shih Tzu, am not!"

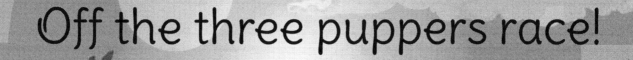

Off the three puppers race!

Sir Andouille yells,
"Dachshund through
the woods!"

Pugsleys asks, "did you say dashund through the woods?"

Sir Andouille mumbles, "I know it is said dahks-hund you pugly mug."

Over rivers
and mountain tops
the three companions
trot!

The knights three
arrive at
Fortress Furball
for their final stop.

Skitter and Scatter stand on high alert,

watching for enemies atop their perch.

Scatter dashes to inform his king of the arrival of the knights three,

while Skitter taunts
the knights looking for
a fight!

Scatter hisses to King Napolean, "my liege, it appears our enemies have cleared the meowntains for the meowment."

"You are barking up the wrong tree," King Napolean angrily shouts!

Scatter and Skedaddle join the battle.

Sir Pugsley repugnantly growls and snarls.

Clearly overpowered by the brave knights,

King Napolean commands the cats to flee from Fortress Furball.

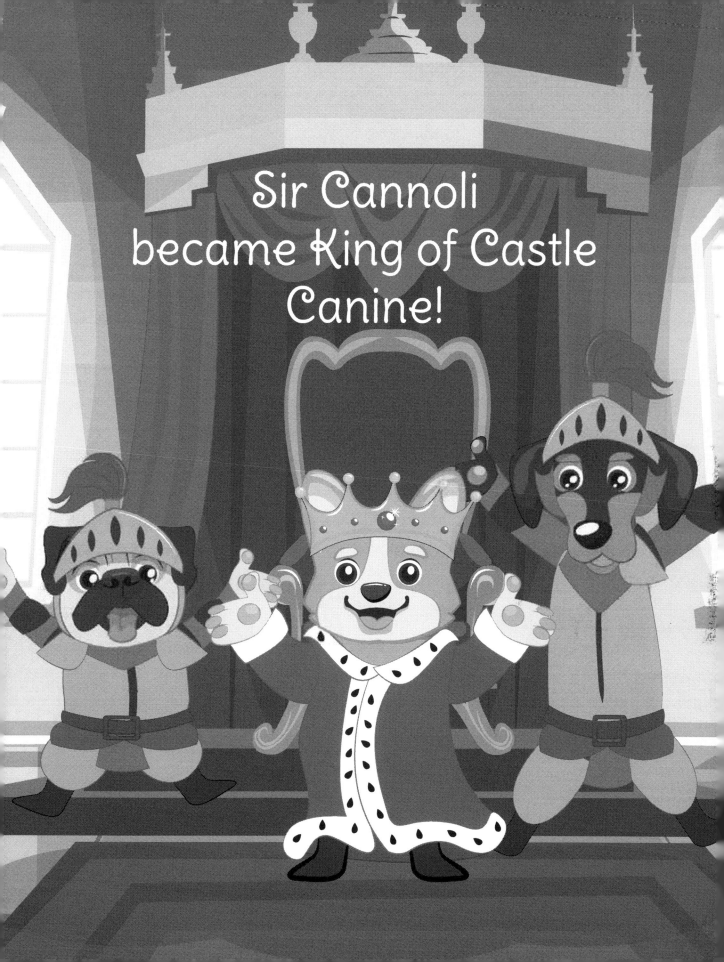

Stay pawsitive
and anything is pawsible!

Made in the USA
Columbia, SC
23 July 2020